Written by Dr. Amy West
Illustrated by Okan Bulbul

ISBN: 978-1-957922-63-8
Edition: December 2022

For all inquiries, please contact us at:
info@puppysmiles.org

To see more of our books, visit us at:
www.PuppyDogsAndIceCream.com

This book is given with love...

To: _____

From: _____

It's Okay to Feel Sad

A foreword by Clinical Psychologist, Dr. Amy West

Sadness is a very normal emotion for children to experience and its presence in daily life should be respected and valued. While sadness may feel uncomfortable and difficult to manage, it is a critical part of our children's human experience. Often children are taught to hide, suppress, or ignore their sad feelings but in fact, their sad feelings should be expressed, acknowledged, and validated. It is then that these feelings can be effectively processed and used to make helpful observations and decisions, or to solve problems.

This book presents an easy and effective approach to learning to manage sad feelings differently - children are encouraged to acknowledge and express the sad feelings they have, identify where the feeling comes from (if they can), break it down into pieces so that they can better understand it, and then apply coping strategies – whether that's accepting and waiting for the sadness to pass, or using active problem-solving. The key to helping children have a healthy relationship with sadness is to reinforce the message that sadness is not a bad or dangerous feeling. It doesn't need to be "fixed", in fact in many cases it cannot be fixed. Sadness can provide important learning experiences for children and parents, and it provides opportunities for problem-solving and growth. It is a critical developmental task for children to learn to tolerate difficult feelings and know that while they cannot always be made to disappear, emotions (whether good or bad) are always temporary experiences. Thus, sadness will always resolve eventually whether children actively cope with it or just acknowledge and honor its presence and let it pass.

In this book, children and parents will learn that there are methods for acknowledging, expressing, and coping with sadness that help normalize its experience as a necessary part of life and encourage children to develop a capacity to feel sadness and learn from it without becoming overwhelmed and impaired.

Sometimes your life, though often bright,
Feels dull or dark, it's true.
When something tough can trip you up,
It's normal to feel blue.

It comes when least expected,
We may not reckon why.
Some days, we frown, and we get down,
Some days, we might just cry.

Sadness impacts all of us,
The old, the strong - that's right!
Dads and Moms, most everyone,
Have shed a tear at night.

Life is full of ups and downs,
Emotions play a part.
It's okay to feel this way,
It shows what's in your heart.

The only thing we can control,
Is how we view each day.
A bumpy road or heavy load,
Will often come your way.

Perhaps, you weren't invited,
To a party last weekend...
You made a mess, you failed a test,
Or argued with a friend.

Yes, sadness can take over,
Can make you feel alone...
Or mope about, perhaps act out,
Like you are on your own.

All of us can sometimes feel,
Sad, or blue, or down.
But there's a way to change your day,
And turn around that frown.

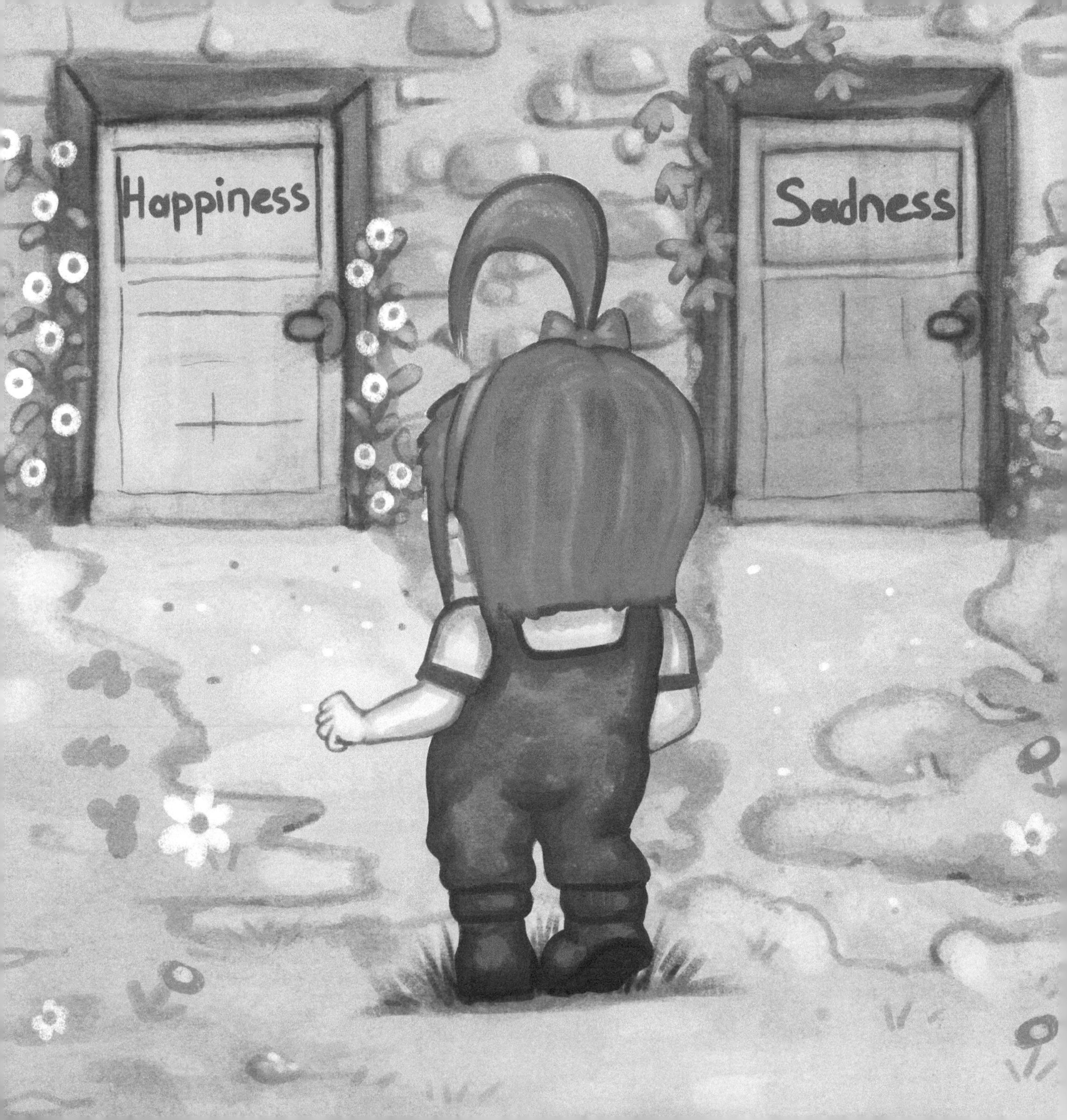
Happiness
Sadness

STEP

1

Acknowledge your sad feelings,
As they travel through your heart.
To decrease stress, speak out, express...
You can draw, or write, to start.

SORROWFUL. DEPRES
S. MISERABLE
DOWNCA
SAD. RE
UNHAPPY - DOWN. DES

STEP
2

Identify the feeling,
Think hard to find the cause.
You may not know, but feelings grow,
Count slow and take a pause.

When something is a mystery,
It's scary and unknown.
By sharing what's upsetting you,
You'll see you're not alone.

STEP
3

How do you tackle tricky things?
No single way is right.
A problem's large 'til you're in charge,
Start small and hold on tight.

Break the problem into bits,
So each part can be addressed.
A smaller task is handled fast,
You'll find you feel less stressed.

STEP

4

Think of sadness as a light switch,
That flips from off to on.
You feel this way, and that's okay,
Each darkness has a dawn.

No storm can last forever,
Though some storms feel they do.
Eventually, the sun breaks free –
You'll find your own path through.

There's always a tomorrow,
A chance to start anew.
You're not alone in this cyclone,
Your friends are there for you.

Seek out a resolution,
There's always one to find.
Don't stay in bed, you'll lose your head,
You can take back your mind.

What you're feeling's very normal,
You can use your mental might...
Every day, construct a way,
To focus on the bright.

Think of something happy,
Take your puppy on a walk...
Sing along to silly songs,
Or hug your mom and talk.

See, sadness is important,
We learn from how we feel.
It isn't bad to say you're sad,
It's how we start to heal.

Your heart just needs some patching,
I'm here to help you sew.
We'll get through this together...
You're loved more than you know!

Claim your FREE Gift!

 Visit:

PDICBooks.com/Gift

Thank you for purchasing

Today, I Feel...

Sad

and welcome to the Puppy Dogs & Ice Cream family.
We're certain you're going to love the little gift
we've prepared for you at the website above.

CPSIA information can be obtained
at www.ICGtesting.com
Printed in the USA
BVHW010711020323
659538BV00002B/12